YOUR BRIDGE TO HISTORY

SECOND EDITION

A Black Votes Matter Initiative
"Face to Face with Black History Tour"
Children's Book

PORTIA LOVE & PRESTON LOVE, JR.
ILLUSTRATED BY **REGINA JEANPIERRE**

Dedicated to the Memory of
Pastor George Keys

Past chaperone and Chaplain of the Tour

From Preston:

Thank you to my wife, Martha Parker Love,
Supervisor of Women, Nebraska First Jurisdiction

Published by Preston Publishing
www.BlackVotesMatterUSA.com

Library of Congress data on file with the Publisher.

Hardcover ISBN: 978-0-9964464-9-5
Paperback: 978-0-9964464-0-2

Illustrations: Regina Jeanpierre
Design and Production: Concierge Marketing Inc.

Printed in the United States of America
10 9 8 7 6 5 4 3 2 1

Hi! My name is Caleb. I am 15 years old and I am a high school student in Omaha, Nebraska.

Last year I was nominated by my youth group to attend a Tour that was put on by a man named Preston Love, Jr.

Mr. Love founded an organization called **Black Votes Matter**. In thinking about the black youth in his community, as future leaders, Mr. Love recognized that black youth did not know enough about their history, and therefore, themselves. He developed this Tour as a fun and exciting opportunity, but also an intensive learning experience.

Mr. Love's Mission Statement for the Tour
History: Learn It, Respect It, Make It.

Mr. Love planned to take 40 students down South and bring them "face to face" with their past. His goal was to teach them where they come from, where they've been, and to help them develop where they are going—then to bridge the three together.

His dream is to help make black youth into future leaders who know and respect their history.

I have become a leader thanks to the Tour, and now I am going to lead you across the **bridge to history**.

After you read this book, you will become a "Tour alumni" just like me!

There is so much of our history that we have not been taught. Let me share what I learned on our tour.

We left in a big tour bus
and headed South.

Dr. Martin Luther King, Jr.'s
Room at the Lorraine Motel

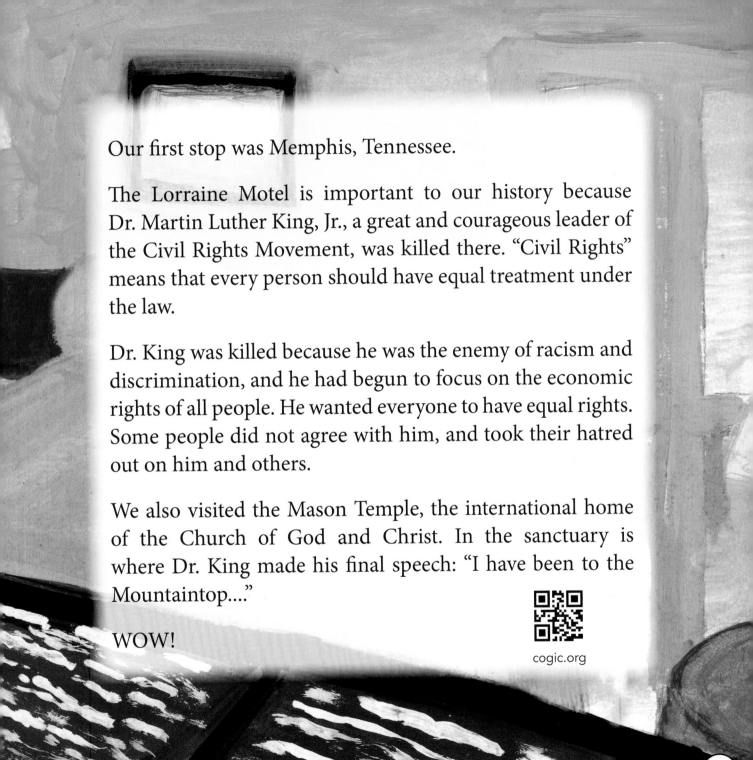

Our first stop was Memphis, Tennessee.

The Lorraine Motel is important to our history because Dr. Martin Luther King, Jr., a great and courageous leader of the Civil Rights Movement, was killed there. "Civil Rights" means that every person should have equal treatment under the law.

Dr. King was killed because he was the enemy of racism and discrimination, and he had begun to focus on the economic rights of all people. He wanted everyone to have equal rights. Some people did not agree with him, and took their hatred out on him and others.

We also visited the Mason Temple, the international home of the Church of God and Christ. In the sanctuary is where Dr. King made his final speech: "I have been to the Mountaintop...."

WOW!

cogic.org

WHITE

COLORED

Not so long ago in the South, black people had to drink out of separate water fountains. There was a nice clean fountain for white people, and a dirty, rusty one for black people.

Fountains were labeled for "white" and "colored".

SIXTEENTH STREET BAPTIST CHURCH

SUNDAY SCHOOL

9:30 AM

WORSHIP SERVICE

SUNDAY 10:45 AM

JOIN US THIS WEEK

www.16thstreetbaptist.org

BLACK VOTES MATTER

Journal

Next, we went to Birmingham, Alabama. When I entered the 16th Street Baptist Church, I couldn't believe such a horrible thing happened there. In 1963, this church was bombed and several young girls were killed. They were with their parents, who were often at the church to fight for Civil Rights, Voting Rights, and to stand up against discrimination.

While we were in Birmingham, we learned about Voting Rights. Here's how they explained it to us:

I've got some jelly beans. They are red, yellow, blue, and green. Which color do you like? When you tell me your choice, you vote for one of the colors. That's voting. Everybody should have the right to choose their own color jelly bean— and to vote. Don't you agree?

The Voting Rights Act of 1965 was designed to make it easier for blacks and other people of color to vote.

Before this Act was signed and put into law, black people in some parts of the United States were forced to pay a poll tax, take a literacy test, and overcome other obstacles (including violence) before they were allowed to vote. This process kept many blacks from voting. The Voting Rights Act made all of those practices illegal.

The next day we went to Selma, Alabama. We visited the Voting Rights Museum and Institute, and then we crossed the Edmund Pettus Bridge.

Until the 1960s, black people were not allowed to vote. Before the Voting Rights Act was signed, there was a Voting Rights march from Selma, Alabama, to Montgomery, Alabama. The goal of the march was to get black people registered to vote.

The first march was called "Bloody Sunday" because law enforcement beat nonviolent protesters as they tried to cross the bridge. There were two more marches. The marches were victorious with the passing of the Voting Rights Act five months later.

The Pettus Bridge is unique. It is the only landmark that has gone from honoring white supremacy to becoming a great monument to racial equality. It has become a bridge to our history.

Edmund Pettus Bridge

On the next day, we went to Montgomery, Alabama, where Rosa Parks is honored.

Rosa Parks refused to give up her seat on the bus to a white person and was arrested for it. Her arrest set off a protest of the city buses that helped to propel the Civil Rights Movement.

Dr. Martin Luther King, Jr., helped to set up a boycott—black people were asked not to ride the bus, and they didn't. The protest lasted a long time, at great personal sacrifice to the black community.

The boycott was successful. As a result, the bus company almost went out of business, and they could no longer make a black person give up their seat to a white person.

Slave Trade Statues
at Equal Justice
Initiative

While in Montgomery, we also visited the Equal Justice Initiative, which documents the black children, women, and particularly men who lost their lives via lynching.

We learned something important about our history, but we cried there, too.

After an emotional day in Montgomery, we had a wonderful Black Votes Matter Tour Barbecue that night. It brought us closer together and was fun like a picnic.

Someone said they only got one chicken wing! I laughed so hard about that. I had more than one because I had a plateful! They must have been too late getting there.

21

Every day of the tour, we wrote about our experiences in our journals. This gave us time to think and talk about everything we had done and seen that day.

The journaling sessions really helped us get everything out of our heads and onto paper.

The King Center

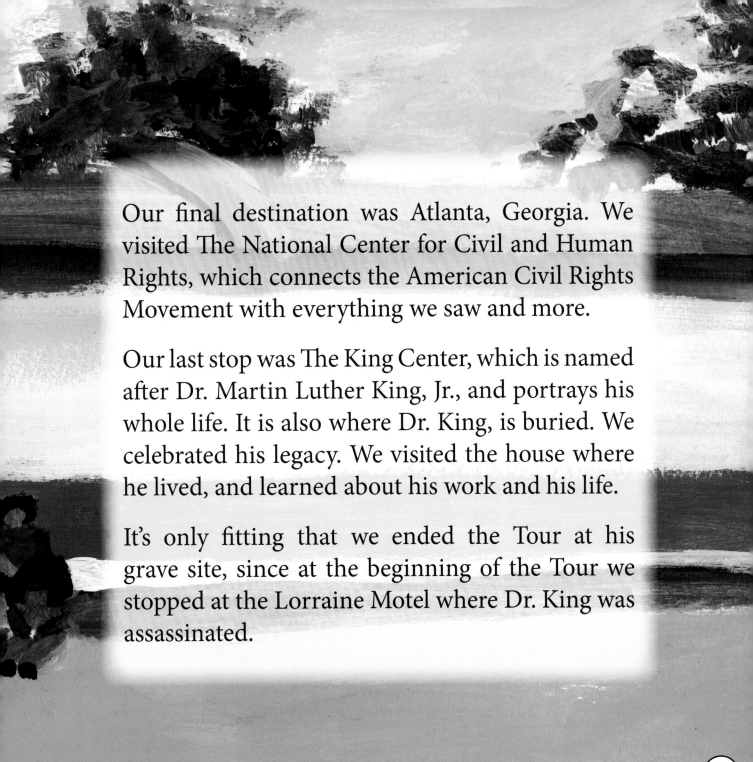

Our final destination was Atlanta, Georgia. We visited The National Center for Civil and Human Rights, which connects the American Civil Rights Movement with everything we saw and more.

Our last stop was The King Center, which is named after Dr. Martin Luther King, Jr., and portrays his whole life. It is also where Dr. King, is buried. We celebrated his legacy. We visited the house where he lived, and learned about his work and his life.

It's only fitting that we ended the Tour at his grave site, since at the beginning of the Tour we stopped at the Lorraine Motel where Dr. King was assassinated.

Scan this QR code with a smart phone to see portions of the Tour documentary.

Those are some of my favorite highlights of our Tour. I hope you have learned something. Every day, Mr. Love told us,

"History: Learn It, Respect It, Make It."
Now it's your turn—go make history!

Preston Love Jr.'s
———— Principles of Living ————

Believe in:

Self

Family

Community

Personal Dream(s)

Ability to Succeed

Realize:

You are loved, you are needed
(by family, community)

Every human receives gifts

The Nevers:

Burn a bridge

Fail to pay a debt
(shows good character)

Give up (quit)

Take Responsibility:

History:
Learn It, Respect It, Make It.

Learn about your community,
your culture, your history.

Lead yourself
(and others will follow)

THE BLACK VOTES MATTER
Institute of Community Engagement 501c(3)

THE "FULL" EXPERIENCE
For Information:
BVM Annual Tour
Ginosko/BVM micro-learning Tutorials
Lectures/Workshops/Seminars
Books by Preston Love Jr.

CONTACT:
Email: prestonlovejr@gmail.com
WEB: BlackvotesmatterUSA.com
Address: 2422 Lake Street
Omaha, NE 68111
Phone: 402-905-9305

THE "FACE TO FACE WITH BLACK HISTORY TOUR"

Black Votes Matter Youth Initiative for the Development of Future Leaders

The seed for the Black Votes Matter Youth Initiative was planted as a response to the lack of knowledge about black history and the Civil Rights Movement. In order for our youth to become effective leaders, they must learn and have respect for their own history. The Tour was designed to address this void.

THE TOUR DESIGN

The design of the Tour is intensive, intentional, and focused, notwithstanding the limitations of the time available (one week). The Tour begins with the venue in Memphis where Dr. Martin Luther King, Jr., delivered his last speech before he was assassinated. The Tour flows into Alabama and discovers many of the iconic events that shaped the entire Civil Rights Movement, in which Dr. King was a key figure. The Tour does not overlook the fact that although Dr. King was central to the movement, there were many other leaders—national and local—as well as grassroots people, events, and circumstances that shaped the entire Civil Rights Movement. Our Tour through Birmingham, Tuskegee, Montgomery, Selma, and the Edmund Pettus Bridge attempts to capture the work of Dr. King and others, and the essence of the Civil Rights Movement. The Tour culminates in Atlanta, where Dr. King was put to rest, but we also capture evidence of the pain and victories in Atlanta. Since its inception, the Tour has been significantly enhanced to include:

1. More pre-Tour activities that focus on local and Nebraska black history.

2. Marvelous video tutorials are available on both laptop and mobile phones, which are used to prepare the participants prior to each day's activities. The tutorials include videos, commentary, and links to educational references, both written and visual.

3. Daily surveying to assess the impact of each day's Tour. Participants gather to reflect, journal, and discuss.

POST-TOUR ACTIVITIES

After the Tour is complete, a comprehensive report is prepared chronicling the feedback from the students about the Tour, the venue stops, and the result of the aggregate surveys.

1. The students are invited to participate in an essay contest geared towards their response to some aspect of the Tour. Winners are awarded a financial stipend as a prize as well as appropriate recognition.

2. Student alumni are urged to participate in an annual Black Votes Matter Service Project.

3. Continued interaction between Black Votes Matter and the student alumni, including mentoring, resources, and speaking opportunities.

4. Future plans to develop the aforementioned tutorials into continuing educational units (CEU).

It should be noted that all expenses are paid for the student participants; this includes the transportation, lodging, venue costs, fees, and food. The students are chosen from nominations made by various youth organizations. Once chosen, student participants become great proponents of diversity. The Tour participants are made up of various races, religions, genders, ethnicities, and they come from different high schools.

We thank the scores of donors who contribute to the expenses of the Tour with special recognition to the Sherwood Foundation, The Weitz Family Foundation, and Omaha Community Foundation's African American Unity Fund.

NOTE: We acknowledge the importance of the leadership and events of Mississippi and other states. On prior tours, time did not allow for visits to every significant location.